FRAGRANCE OF RELATIONSHIP

STORIES

SHASHI PATHAK

Dedicated

To

my dear father

Mr. Chandrapal Sharma 'Rasik Hathrasi'

Mrs. Shashi Pathak

Contents

Contents

Preface

Smt. Shashi Pathak is a senior litterateur of Hindi literature. You have been involved in writing work for four decades. She has published two story collections and one children's novel in Hindi and one children's novel in English. A story collection written in English literature"fragrance of relationship" is her second story collection, in which 16 excellent stories and 16 short stories have been included.

All the stories and short stories of this collection are also seen trying to dissolve sweetness in relations by removing social and family inequalities and bitterness.

I extend my heartfelt greetings that the writings of Mrs. Shashi Pathak, by creating such excellent literature in Hindi and in English, remove social and family evils and keep mixing sweetness in mutual relations.

With Best Wishes:
Acharya Neeraj shastri
34/2 Lajpat Nagar,
Mathura

Acknowledgements

FROM WRITER'S PEN

I would like to share my view that there is a writer within every person, who is certainly affected by events, nature and environment around them and express their reaction through their own ways. May be- poetry, story, essay, art, music or through conversation.

I have been sensitive since childhood. My father Shri Chandrapal Sharma alias 'Rasik Hathrasi' writes heart touching poems. I was inspired to write from him only. I participated in many school and college level cultural programmes. Writing for school magazine, delivering speech on functions and remaining on the top of the list in debate competitions was a very usual thing for me. So along with studies there was always an environment of literature around me. Whenever any incident or anything influenced me, I expressed it in the form of story.

I was married to Sri Dinesh Pathak of Rampur, immediately after completing my postgraduation. By the grace of God, he was a reputed writer. His compositions got place in magazines of different level. And his stories were relayed from different centres of radio.

It is true that I wrote before marriage also, but had never sent any of my writings for publications. with the proper guidance of husband, my compositions started getting place in different magazines and also relayed from radio centres.

Here in Mathura, there was environment of literature at home. After my husband came from office, his writer friends visited my house and literary discussions in the evening were frequent, this undoubtedly improved my writings. My husband always inspired me to write better. My collection of stories "Fragrance of relationship" which consists of 15 short stories is before you.

There are many relations in the society- Husband-wife, mother-son, brother-sister, father-son and many others. We all are related to each other in one or another way. Relationship has its distinct fragrance. Many people and conditions try to make their conditions bitter. I have always made an effort to remove this bitterness through my stories, whenever I am confronted with such situations. Most of the stories of this collection are based on similar themes. Your reaction will give the result of my effort that is, to what extent I have been successful in doing this.

At the end, I would like to thank Mrs. Urmi Krishna ji for writing this preface and publisher Sri Sanjeev Gupta ji. I also want to thank all my acquaintances, friends, writers and scholars who have directly and indirectly, provided their support in publication of this collection of stories. And last but not the least, I want to thank Mrs. Vandana Asthana for translating this collection of stories into English.

Shashi Pathak
28 Sarang Vihar
Mathura-281006
UP (Bharat)

CHAPTER ONE

SUPPORT

Savitri Devi got up with the ring of call bell on the door. As she opened the door, Juhi was standing on the gate, burdened with a bag, face blushing red with the heat of sun. "Grand ma! You get late in opening the door. You know I am so hungry!"

Grandmother had served her food on the dining table by the time Juhi washed her hands and changed her clothes. After having her lunch, Juhi sat for doing homework. After sometime when the sun went down, she went to play, as usual.

Savitri glanced at the watch after Juhi went to play. It was not yet 6 in the evening. She came to the doorstep. Children were playing joyfully in the park, just in front of her house. She kept watching their game forsome time and then coming inside put the tea pan on the gas.

Savitri took out the album from almirah and sat on the sofa. She started turning over the leaves of the album. She was growing more and more nostalgic as she recalled days of forty years before, filled with many memories-- some bitter, some sweet. On the next leaf, there was her photograph with her dear husband, just after two years of marriage. She was ashamed as the happiness on her face revealed in the photo came to her memory. How happy they were, as they were expecting a new member in their family! She sank into deep thoughts.

Turning over the leaves of the album, suddenly Savitri's conscience groaned with pain and the scene shadowed her mind, when Sudhir's father was lying on the bed in the hospital. This was the photograph just before the road accident. Savitri burst into tears. Some days after his death, her mother-in-law also expired and she remained alone in this big world. But she was compelled to live, for her little son, Sudhir. What a great difficulty she faced in bringing up Sudhir! Remembering all these, she shivered from inside. Sudhir started feeling his mother's problem when he grew up. He used to sit beside his mother and used to ask many questions curiously. She tried to answer his questions in such a way that his soft heart might not be hurt. But circumstances made the child more mature than his age. He could understand that his mother tailored clothes to pay his fees. Savitri worked hard day and night. Her only aim was to make her son, Sudhir, an educated and able man.

Her dreams came true after a few years. Her joy knew no bounds when Sudhir got job as bank manager. Nice marriage proposals started coming for Sudhir. Savitri wanted to take rest after getting Sudhir married as she was now tired. But experiences of life always created a fear in her mind. She always thought of Prashant, the only son of her sister was enticed by his wife and lived separately. Her sister had also sacrificed her life to make her son, doctor. She had to sell all her property for making him a doctor. He left for America with his educated doctor wife immediately after marriage, leaving his weeping mother behind. Sending her some money from America, he thought that he was free from her debt. He perhaps could never understand that mother's debt cannot be paid in money.

Savitri started thinking that she would not marry her son to any qualified girl. She shared her mind with Sudhir too, that his wife would be according to his choice, but she should not be educated. She should be cultured so that she might take your care as well as mine. I don't want anything else. Well qualified daughters-in-law cannot give us these things. As per her wish, Sudhir's wife was beautiful, polite and expert in household works. Savitri got a great delight with her care. The daughter-in-law did all the household works happily and Inspite of being busy, she took her complete care. Daughter-in-law was far better than Savitri's expectations. Savitri was satisfied. Savitri felt proud when her neighbour,Kanta praised her [Savitri's] daughter-in-law saying she was so lucky to get such a well-behaved daughter-in-law. Kanta always regrated on selection of her own daughter-in-law, as she wasproudy due to being a bit educated.

Some years later, she was blessed with a grand-daughter,this added a feather in her cap. Her squeal throughout the day, made Savitri overjoyed whole day. The baby girl kept her busy and one year passed. We made great preparations for Juhi's first birthday. The whole house was filled with the essence of the delicious dishes. All the guests and relatives started coming. We were waiting for Sudhir, to come from office. The weather was very pleasant. Cool breeze was blowing. But suddenly there were dark clouds in the sky and heavy rain started. Lightning and thunder was terrifying them. Electricity was gone. The house that was shining a moment ago turned dark. Their anxiety for Sudhir became intense.

After sometime, rain stopped, clouds dispersed. Lights were on, but with this there was complete darkness in her life. She screamed at the repetition of the same incident in her life.

It was a bolt from the blue. Sudhir's accident, his tormenting body in the hospital.............everything was dark before her eyes. Her daughter-in-law fainted, seeing her husband's condition. She turned stone, staring in emptiness. Savitri had suffered so much in her life that her heart had turned stone.

But how will this soft-hearted daughter bear this trouble! She was regretting at her decision of marrying Sudhir to an illiterate girl, otherwise she could earn her livelihood doing job in place of Sudhir. Now who will ask this illiterate girl!

"Mother" Sudhir called as he came to senses.

"My son! What happened to you?"

"Mother I don't have much time. I had told lie and I beg excuse for that." Sudhir said groaning with pain.

"Mother, it was a lie that your daughter-in-law is illiterate. She is qualified like me." Saying this, his head tumbled one side and tears started flowing persistently.

The ring of call bell at the gate, brought her to the present. Wiping her tears, she kept the album in the Almirah and went to open the door. Daughter-in-law had returned from the bank and behind her was Juhi who had also come back from the school.

"Grandma, had you slept again?"

"Naughty girl! Keep quiet." Daughter-in-law rebuked her with love and Savitri smiled. Then she went in the kitchen and brought tea.

"What is this maa! I have told you several times, not to take troubles, I can do these things myself."

Her sweet behaviour compelled Savitri to think about her past decision. "If she had been illiterate, would she have been able to support me. She is not at all proud of her education."

Many times, our conviction is so baseless. She was deeply obliged to her daughter-in-law.

"What is the problem dear? You work hard throughout the day- household work, then your job and my care. Don't you get tired?" Savitri said, looking into her eyes.

Daughter-in-law embraced her. She could just pronounce with her chocked throat "Maa!"

Savitri too hugged her whole heartedly.

***

CHAPTER TWO

SPIDER WEB

I had never thought even in dream that the seeds, I had sown would one day transform into such a giant evil tree that it will crush the existence of young trees and I will have to watch it like a mute audience.

How to uproot it? Its roots have entered so deep that it is very difficult to uproot it. Now it's going to bear fruit too. Tasting this fruit will also be harmful. Let alone eat it completely.

But what can be done now. Nobody will believe me even if I make him understand. And it is indeed difficult to believe all this, because it was I only who instilled all these things in the minds of mother, father and society, now they are unable to deny it.

Now they have taken for granted that my in laws are not good people. They think that I am helpless and it is the irony of an Indian lady. My parents are accusing my in-laws as they are unaware of reality.

My sixty percent burnt body in the hospital ward was enough to prove the letter I had written to my parents a few years before. God knows, how it all happened!

Just then voice of sister "Madam I have to bandage your wounds." Broke the continuity of my thoughts. Nurse departed after doing her duty and as per the rules of the hospital. Queue of visitors started meeting their patients.

Along with my parents, my in laws, husband and children also hadcame. My children were looking at me from a distance fearfully. The doctor came on round and said, "Don't worry, she is out of danger."

My parents and in laws were sitting like enemies and were firm on their views.

My father handed the divorce papers in my hand- "Put your signature on it."

I looked at the papers and then towards the faces of husband and innocent children.

"No, never, I can't do this."

"But you can die? This time we were lucky that you escaped otherwise these butchers_______." Father burst out with choked throat.

"Stop it, papa. Don't blame them." I cried out. I was deeply perturbed. I looked into the eyes of my husband, and I could see ocean of love for me in his eyes. It never reflected any intention of hurting me. Everyone went after sometime and I was again alone. A whirlpool of thought began to swirl in my mind again. I am the cause of this difference between my parents and in laws . I must end up this difference. But will my effort change this attitude.

With a deep sigh I began to curse those days when I had sown this seed of hatred between the two families. It was the marriage of my younger sister. Papa had arranged more than his capacity. She was 9 years younger to me. Nine years before when I was married, I was not given so much in dowry. From here started my jealousy and a competition.

I started torturing my parents, sometime through letters and sometime going to them personally, demanding different things like scooter, T.V, refrigerator etc.... in the name of husband and in laws. Father was often furious whenever I told them thatmy in laws tortured me on not taking these things with me, although it was all lie, that I told them all the time. And I always forced them to fulfil the demand. Father arranged all these things for me taking loans, just to see me happy. When asked the reason of bringing these things by my in laws and husband, my father thought it their double policy, and used to say sarcastically, "It is just for my daughter's happiness."

But one day, this incident took place when I suddenly went to thekitchen to prepare tea in the morning. No sooner did I light the matchstick than I was surrounded by flames. My husband was sleeping and mother-in-law busy in her work. Hearing my cry all of them came there and my husband was also affected by the fire while saving me.

Later it was discovered that the gas pipe was cut off by a rat and gas leaked and filled in the whole kitchen. But I failed to notice this leakage.

An acute headache started. The wounded burnt parts were paining. I have got result of my owndeed. But what is their mistake for which they are being punished. They would never have thought of this sin, let alone committing the mistake.

All the incidents of the time when I was new in this house started coming to my mind. I was overwhelmed with affectionate behaviour of in laws. I got so much love and affection in my in laws' house that I forgot my own house. Two years passed and then Sneha came in our life and made it happier. Time was passing joyously but bad time fell its evil sight on our joy. Not of time, but it was all due to me, that's why such mischief came in my mind.

She sank into deep sleep, thinking about the way to come out of this whirlpool.

"No, I will never sign these papers."

"But dear daughter, see what they have done with you? Do you want to be trapped in this net again?"

"Why don't you believe me papa, the fact is not what you are thinking. This is all a lie. Nobody ever tortured me. I kept telling lies to you, so that I could get these luxury items from you. Whatever I am telling is true, papa. I am responsible for this all."

"No, we can never accept this. You are uselessly lying to protect these cruel people. But we have also decided to put them in the jail. We are still alive and you should not think yourself alone."

My whole body began to feel senseless and tears started flowing from my eyes, at father's obstinate behaviour. I was regretting at my own mistake. Father came and sat at my side, thinking that I was becoming emotional. But my eyes were searching my husband and children.

Just then I noticed that my husband was standing outside the ward, holding Sneha's finger and Yugal in his lap.

I don't know from where I got the power, I snatched the divorce papers from papa and tore it into many small pieces and wept bitterly clinging to husband's leg.

Papa woke me up. My tears were not stopping. Just like my dream papa was sitting by my side, moving his hand on my forehead.

"Dear this nightmare will keep haunting you until you get rid of these people. I have completed these papers. You have only to put your sign on it."

"Give it to me papa." Taking the divorce papers in my hand, I tore it into pieces, just as I did in my dream.

***

CHAPTER THREE

STIGMA OF PAST

Everything around was heart breaking, as if Lord Shiva has made a resolution to destroy the creation in the form of earthquake. There was an outcry all around. Many houses were being destroyed and the search dogs were ransacking the ruins smelling everywhere.

After that there were police and social workers who were taking out the dead bodies from the heap of ruin and performing their funeral, carrying the wounded people to the hospital.

The devoted social worker, sister Suza, had forgotten herself and was busy in caring forthose earthquakeaffected people- Bandaging their wounds. Serving people was her only aim. She too groaned with the people crying with pain, seemed like a Goddess to these people.

"Sister, Doctor Smith has called you immediately." Informed the ward boy. Completing the bandage of the patient on bed number 10, she reported to the doctor. "Sir, had you called me?"

"Yes, sister a complicated case, make preparation for operation."

"Yes sir."

Whatever was happening, compelled to think that there is God somewhere. Everything happens as per his wish.

She had lost her only son who had just fallen off the cot while this small child has come out alive after being buried in the ruin for so many days, when nothing is left, houses, animals, property.. in this violent earthquake. The child was on oxygen support and doctor was trying to bring back life into her. As she started crying, all became happy.

"Sister, take care of this child and in case of any emergency, inform me at once."

"Ok sir."

Sister Suza patted the child on her back and with this, she stopped crying and fell asleep.

Sister Suza was expressing surprise on God's behaviour. He may take away or give life to anyone. everything is unpredictable about God's decision. Nobody knows what's going to happen the next moment. Now and then, she glanced at the face of the small child and sank into her past.

The incident is of four years back. Everyone in the house was overwhelmed with joy. The whole house was decorated with lights, that it seemed like day. We came back from the church friends and relatives were coming to congratulate. Now it was the turn of meeting her beloved. Her joy knew no bounds.

After a few days, they planned to go to a hill station. Loving partner and pleasant breeze did not let her feel how far the place was. Circular roads, tall trees of Deodar and Chinar and above the cloud laden sky made them feel that they were roaming in heaven.

Each day, having our breakfast we went out from the guest house and then after lunch and got lost in the depth of beauty of nature. Boating, roaming near waterfall or watching beauty of the town hand in hand. When one month passed, they never realised.

While returning too they were enjoying the same scene. She was wandering in the heaven like pleasure, then a turn came in her life that ruined her whole life. Their car struck against a bus coming from the opposite direction and went on sliding down. She became unconscious, by the time she came to senses, her whole world was snatched from her by the cruel hands of time. Her husband, died on the spot. But she had to struggle, so she saved. She shivered to see her changed life, but Dr. Smith compelled her to live for the sake of her unborn child. He gave her job of nurse in his hospital, so that she could earn her livelihood.

After sometime, she gave birth to a son, who was exactly looking like his father, hence she named him Anuroop. She tried to fill gap in her life, seeing her child playing. Anuroop became her life support. But this joy was also not acceptable to her fate. She had gone to hospital, leaving Anuroop with maid. She was just about to return from the hospital when the maid came running and said, "Mam Anuroop has gone unconscious falling from bed." She went running but till then, everything was over. Her support of life had left her alone in this world. Once again, her fate deceived her. She felt that nature was mocking at her fate. She was very angry at God's judgement, but what could she do.

Child's cry woke her up and she came back to present. She picked up the child, changed her wet clothes and looked at the watch. It was already dawn.

After sometime, Dr. Smith came on round, "How is her activity sister, pulse?"

"Everything was quite ok sir."

"Good, but______"

"What sir?"

"There is no one alive in her family. All the members died in earthquake. She too was carried away by the sorrow of the child. A thought of adopting the child came to her mind, but the next moment she halted thinking she would also be taken away, as her luck never favours her.

Dr. Smith turned back, "What happened sister?"

"Nothing, sir!"

"I feel you are not well, Go and take rest."

Coming home, she thought about the child. A conflict was going on between her terrified mind and affection for the child. She would get a leave only when she is quite well. Onceagain a sort of affection cropped up in her mind.

This child is alive Inspite of this destruction, perhaps to make her life cheerful again.

I shall see, everything will happen as per God's wish. She will never accept defeat. Once again, she prepared herself.

She had already taken her decision, when she reached the cabin of Dr. Smith. Being busy in his work, he was shocked to see sister Suza there.

"What happened sister? Your duty is over! Are you ok?"

"Yes, doctor I am quite ok. I have decided to adopt this child. I will take her care."

Tears came out from her eyes and bedewed her cheeks. She did not know whether her decision was to bear one more pain or get pleasure from this child.

***

CHAPTER FOUR

UNIQUE EXPERIMENT

Daddy answered in response to the knock at the door.

"Come in, door is open."

It was Kapoor uncle on the door. He came in and sat on a chair that mummy had placed right near him and turned to bring snacks.

"No sister, mother has already prepared breakfast, but one of her hands got burnt while frying poori in the pan. You know she is very old and hence her eyesight has deteriorated."

"Did you not apply any ointment?" mother asked concernedly.

"That's why I have come here. Neha has kept Burnol somewhere and it is not found anywhere."

Yes, why not, I am going myself and apply it on her hand." And she went to Kapoor uncle's house.

Just after mother departed, father said to uncle, "Why do you let her do so much work?"

"What can I do? Mother doesn't allow me to keep maid servant."

"I am not telling you to keep maid. I am telling you to marry and bring a person who will fulfil everyone's need."

"You are right friend. But I am afraid, how would she treat Neha, being her step-mother."

"You should not fear of this. Every girl is not same. Have you ever felt that Ratna, my wife, is Shashi's step mother?"

Father's words shocked Kapoor uncle. He said excitedly, "What do you say Mr. Sharma! Neither you ever told me nor I have ever notice any such Bhabhiji's behaviour. You had told that your first wife had died, but I never knew that Shashi is your first wife's daughter."

"Oh! You have come back. Did you apply medicine on her hand? Is it still paining?" father said, changing the topic as mother entered.

"Yes, it is badly wounded and pain is too much."

"O.K Kapoor you go home. It's time for the office too. I will come to see mother while going to office."

"Good morning mother! how did you get your hand burnt?" father asked going near her cot.

"It's old age dear, a bit oil splashed and sprinkled on my hand."

"That's I say, get Kapoor married. There must be someone to take care in your old age. Kapoor goes to office and Neha leaves for school. You remain alone the whole day."

"You are right dear, but_______" she got in a dilemma.

Just then Kapoor entered room and cut him short, "Mother today Mr. Sharma gave a new information that Bhabhi ji is Shashi's step mother."

She was shocked to hear this, "Is this right dear? That's why Shashi is quite different from other children. But I never discussed the matter, lest you should feel bad."

"Then what do you say about Kapoor's marriage mother?" we shall bring girl from a cultured family and you will see that she will give more affection to Neha than even a real mother."

"Yes, you are right, but you persuade Kapoor."

"That I will do but you get ready."

"Now dear it's time for your office. You will be late. We shall talk over this matter afterwards." She said carelessly.

Both of them left for the office. Every treatment of hers towards Mr. Sharma was coming in her mind. She remembered the day when he had newly joined the office after his transfer. Shashi was busy in arranging new quarter from morning till evening while other children were playing. She remembered the day of fair in the town, when all children were enjoying the fair but Shashi did not go outside. Mother thought that day too, why she was different from other children of Mr. Sharma. The series of thoughts were coming to end. That day, she had gone to Mr. Sharma's house, his wife was admiring her daughter Rachna for deep interest and talent in stitching and embroidery. She informed that she had registered her in a embroidery centre. But Shashi has no interest in this field. She started linking these things to Ratna as a step-mother for Shashi and again series of thought started striking her mind as-

"If Ratna wanted, Shashi could also learn these things? But the question is, if she wants? But why she should? After all she is her step-mother." With all these thoughts in her mind, she sank into deep sleep.

After waking up she came to my house. Mother welcomed her and asked about her burnt wounds and asked Rachna to bring a glass of water.

"No dear, I don't need" and she sat down. Rachna called from inside, "Mummy see the gram flour batter is proper or not for frying fritter?"

"Don't you teach cooking to Shashi?" asked Mr. Kapoor's mother.

"She is not at all interested in cooking. She always remains busy in books. Today her grandmother has come

so she has gone to market with her. Must be coming."

"What can she do? You just don't teach her anything. She will have to face trouble after marriage."

"She will learn everything when situation comes. Let her relax. After marriage every girl has to work hard."

"How can she learn? You don't want to teach her anything, after all you are her step mother. how can you be her well-wisher." Mother blurt out.

"I am her step-mother? who told you? Someone might have joked." Mummy got puzzled.

"Why will anyone joke on this matter? Don't I see your behaviour towards Shashi? You teach everything to your own daughter Rachna and never to Shashi. Does this not show your step treatment? only study will not carry girl's life."

"No, mother, Shashi is my own child not step." Mummy burst into tears.

"How can I believe you? Has Mr. Sharma told us a lie? Let him come. He will only tell the reality."

Just then daddy entered saying, "Ratna, this was the new experiment."

"Experiment?" mummy said irritatingly.

"I just wanted to see if step mother is really bad or society is bad which start searching the short comings as the word 'step' is connected to a relation."

***

CHAPTER FIVE

TIME

The peon at the gate repeated the name of the next applicant with the ring of bell and indication of clerk inside.

I was shocked to see the face of the next applicant. My face suddenly became firm. The applicant saw towards me and tried to read my facial expression. His face revealed many expressions in a flash of moments and at last it got pale.

Why has this person come ? Has he come to meet me ? his opinion never coincided with me. If he could be some other person but ---- No. Ten years is not such a long time as to forget a face.

Eventoday I remember those years that we spent in Belapur. We felt very strange when father was transferred there. It was a small village, unhygienic all around. There was neither park nor any college. There was only a junior high school. We had to join that school only.

Gradually many of my classmates become friend. But I could never reconcile with Narayana. It was not because of economic disparity between us, he was the son of a rich father while I was the son of a simple government clerk. The main reason of our difference was our different attitude. He always boasted off his riches, high caste and his foreign watch , shoes etc. while I never paid attention to these things.

Narayan's father, Rambabu Singh was the richest person of his village. He was a contractor. Narayan was his only son and very pampered. We were three brothers and sister. Father's income was not enough to meet the demands of the family. No question of luxuries.

Whenever I got a chance to go to Narayan's house with school friends, I always felt myself inferior, seeing the pomp and shaw of his bungalow and high class living. His servants were obedient to him. I felt very strange after coming back from his house. A small room was our bedroom, kitchen and guestroom also.

Many times, Narayan used to speak very harshly on the way to school. One day it started raining while we were going to school. Narayan opened his folding umbrella and told proudly "Your father doesn't love you. My father loves me very much. See what a costly umbrella he has bought for me. This is father's love." I pushed him angrily so forcefully that his forehead dashed against the wall and it started bleeding.

Immediately I came out of my thoughts. The applicant was still standing before me, waiting for my hint to take his seat. I said, "Take your seat".

He thanked me and seated himself on the chair hesitatingly and bent his head down. I carefully observed his face. The mark on his forehead was clearly visible. Now it was sure that the person was no one else but Narayan. I was amazed that the only son of rich contractor, Sri Rambabu Singh had come to apply for a fourth-class job. Time is so powerful and changing. Is he the sameperson who insulted him in the name of poverty and caste. A feeling of realisation started emerging within me. I had got a chance to take revenge. I was feeling proud of myself.

Father was transferred from Belapur after I had passed eighth class. I got my higher education there only. But Narayana's insulting words kept haunting me all the time. So, I too made much effort in studies so that I could became an officer one day. I got the result and I became an officer. After a formal interview of Narayana. I called on the next candidate telling that he would be informed Narayana looked at me with a requestful expression and left the room with folded hands.

But after Narayanaleft the room. I too become disturbed and finished my interview session. I started towards home. On the way I went on thinking about Narayana.

His different phases of life. I was lingering between his proudly attitude of young age to the helpless pleader of that day. I thought, certainly there must be a serious problem in his life.

I sent the appointment letter on his address and started waiting for the day of his joining. Begging permission, he entered my cabin and fell on my feet. " Sir you saved me. I had thought you would not give me a chance, but you are really God."

I got up from my chair and holding him up I said , " Take your seat Narayan. You perhaps did not recognize me."

"No, Sir, I didn't recognize you."

"You are the son of thakur Rambabu Singh of Belapur ?"

" Yes , Sir, but how do you know all this ?"

" Because I am your classmate , Mohan."

" Mohan , you have become a great officer."

" Yes Narayana, but you, in such a miserable condition, I cannot understand anything."

" It's a strange story , how could I keep my proud , if Ravan could not I."

" But still , friend how all this happened ?"

" My proud of wealth opened ways of my destruction. After passing junior high-school , father sent me to town to study in a very good school. I stayed in hostel there and wasted all my money in gambling. I failed in the exam , but my parents were in dark about it. I never understood that I was cheating my parents.

One day suddenly father suffered a big loss in his business and he got a heart attack. We had to sell our bungalow. I became a homeless wanderer.

I left Belapur with mother and started a search for job. Now I am tired. I still remember your words, Mohan that time changes. Excuse me Mohan."

***

CHAPTER SIX

After Darkness

I was in a dilemma having received Prabhat's letter. On the one hand the joy of meeting son , daughter in law and grand- daughter and on the other hand the , memory of their first visit started paining my heart.

Every sound at the door, filled me with excitement as if he had come.A strange happiness clouded her mind since she had heard that her children were coming. Time of wait was seeming very long. Today I was going to get the result of my whole life's sacrifice.

Born and brought up in poverty, I always compromised with my desires. Being good at studies. I could continue my studies on scholarship. I wanted to be a doctor and whenever I went to hospital with father and saw doctors on round, in white uniform , my ambition of being a doctor grew stronger. I always determined to be a doctor but being the eldest among brothers and sisters. I could never raise my voice.

The ring of call bell interrupted the series of my thought perhaps he has come. I got up enthusiastically and opened the door. But the milkman at the door ended all my excitement.

" Madam from today the cost of milk has increased by one rupee" he said , pouring milk in the pan. " It's o.k. , but bring more milk from tomorrow."

" Is anyone coming , madam ?"

" Yes, Prabhat is coming."

" It's a very good news !"

I went into the kitchen and put the milk on the gas burner , thinking that my sorrows are going to end. I never got a space in my life since childhood. I always curbed my desires and gradually all my ambitions were buried , except one wish. I tried to fulfil my ambition. Passed the entrance exam too , but suddenly father had a heart attack and then a second attack. I was compelled to drop my ambition and marry , everyonegave me full love and support in my in laws house but my husband everyday come home , heavily drunk. I had to tolerate all those thingI understood why he married such a poor girl like me.

After two to three months, I conceived and giving him an oath in the name of coming child. I requested him to stop drinking and to my amazement he accepted my proposal. I was very happy but my joy was not for a long time. It was raining very heavily I was feeling very peculiar that day. There was a heavy lightning. It became dark but he did not return. I was filled with so many questions. Suddenly the call bell rang.

Opening the door and was shocked to see my husband badly bleeding in the hands of our neighbour ,Mr.Ram Nath.

" Sister, my friend has left us forever."

I was speechless and became unconscious. Coming to senses I come to know that he died being crushed under a lorry.

I decided to do something to earn my livelihood. I started stitching clothes and then tuitions. I had to bring up Prabhat. Due to lack of money Prabhat's study too suffered

, hence I decided to continue my education.At last I became a lecturer. Now my only aim was to make Prabhat a doctor.

Everything was going accordingly. Prabhat cleared the entrance exam and got admission in the medical college, He got scholarship from government to continue his higher education abroad. I was very happy. My dream was coming true.

A knock at the door , interrupted my thought series.

There was postman at the door, he handed me a telegram. I had a sudden premonition of fear but got relaxed when I read it. It said , “We are reaching India on June 10 in the evening. The clock showed 6.30 p.m.the time was passing. Every moment was seeing very long like ages. Every word in the telegram was arising questions in my mind. But very soon all my anxiety was buried with the message of Prabhat on telephone that he has gone to a hotel , straight from the airport. I reached on the address and looked at Prabhat with a question on my face and responded immediately “ maa actually our house is very small. She may face problem , so..”

Yes , the same house where Prabhat was born and brought up was very small for him today. I came back home with heavy heart , thinking that happiness is not in my lot. Husband left , Prabhat is no more my right , all my struggle for nothing. I was lost in thoughts when the call bell at the door interrupted my thoughts. I got up with a start and opened the door. For my surprise it was Prabhat with his wife and baby.

“ Oh ! You !”

“ Yes mother !” Both touched my feet.

But I was still in a dilemma and asked “ Why didn’t you make an arrangement for her in the hotel ?”

No , mother , now I will open my clinic here only. See maa ! I have learnt to speak Hindi too. Hindi words from the mouth of a foreign daughter – in – law seemed very sweet. I was overwhelmed with joy and taking my granddaughter in my lap , hugged her.

***

CHAPTER SEVEN

Realisation Of Mistake

Many times, we take such decisions in life for which we have to regret later. But at the time of making decision, we feel that we are perfectly right and noones warning affects us.

The same condition I am suffering from. Today it's difficult to believe that I, who was so active and so live hearted person at time is now sitting helplessly and lonely on a wheel chair and afraid of even my own shadow. This is nothing but the result of my single mistake.

Maid standing near me startles me " Madam , why are you weeping ? Did you get any news from Chhavi Didi's in laws house."

" Oh ! nothing like that . I just got nostalgic about some past incidents." I started wiping my tears with the edge of my saree.

Driving my wheel chair, I came to the balcony. Children were busy in playing in the park in front of my house. I moved into long past when I and my husband were sitting on a bench and had totally forgotten that we were in a public park.

" Listen !"He called me slowly.

" Hmm !"

" We shall name our child ' Darpan ' in which you will be able to see my face , OK."

" Why not Chhavi , in which we shall be able to see our impression ?"

" It's alright ! Chhavi or Darpan both mean same."

After two months Chhavi came in our life. My mother-in-law was not happy as she had been dreaming of a grandson. But as the time passed Chhavi became very naughty and my mother-in-law enjoyed her nearness. When she used to take her to school and bring her back from school. Five years passed. Everyone started thinking of another child, Naval said excitedly, "This year our Darpan should come."

" If it does not come true and Chhavi's sisterChhaya comes then ?" I Joked.

" We didn't wish to have more than two children – your Chhavi and my Darpan."

" It's OK , we shall see but after that no issue."

" Agreed" Naval said.

Don't know how these words reached mother's ears. She started a lot of hue and cry and cried that I would put a stop on her lineage. Just to carry on the lineage. I gave birth to five children, then only I was able to see the face of Naval and now this queen will give birth to only two children whenever may be , I want a grandson.

Just to console her I told that I will not do family planning. Then only she stopped crying.

She always lingered around me , giving instructions of what to do and what not to do. After all the day came when I was taken to the nursing home. She was praying before God for Grandson. But fortune had something else in store for me. Chhavi's Chhaya came in the world. She was deeply shocked and got ill and died after sometime.

Naval also became very quiet , but mischievous activities of Chhaya made him cheerful again. Now she had started going to school.

I got angry when one day Naval told , " Ratna , now you get operated."

"No, I have promised mother and I will not do this. I will not hurt her soul. I will fulfil her dream."

" Have you gone mad ? I don't think any difference between son and daughter. As far as mother is concerned , why are you becoming so conservative ?"

" No , Navel, I will not cheat her by breaking my promise" cried out.Naval also got emotional and said , " OK , as you wish."

After some years I again conceived. I was worried about the result. I started living in anxiety and became vexed at small things. Doctor advised for a check-up. Naval agreed with a great difficulty for it.

" If it is found out that the child is a girl , will you get it aborted ?"

" Sure , what will we do of three daughters."

" Don't think like this . May be the child born is male."

Some days after this check-up I suffered from a heavy pain. We went to the doctor. It was diagnosed that there was an infection which developed during the sex determination test doctor advised for operation immediately.

" Doctor, please save my Ratna anyhow."Naval said worriedly.

" Don't worry , we shall try our best." Doctor consoled us.

The child inside the womb died during operation. I was deeply shocked. I had not come out ofthis sorrow when my legs stopped supporting. I cried bitterly.

Naval always consoled me saying everything happens as per god's will. We have two pretty daughters and they are no less than a son.

My daughters Chhavi and Chhaya took the responsibility of whole family along with their studies. But after Chhavi's marriage Naval too left us alone in this world. Chhaya too went abroad to pursue her studies of medical. It's five years , she has been abroad.

Continuous ring of call bell broke my deep thoughtsand I came to present.

" Laxmi ! Laxmi ! see who is at the door." I called her wiping my tears.

" Madam ! our Chhaya has come." Chhaya came and closed my eyes and hugged me warmly.

" Why did you not inform ?"

"Surprise !" She said mischievously

" Now I have come to you forever. Now I shall cure you and never let you live sad. You remained alone for long. I will open my clinic here."

She could perhaps guess my sadness.

"Really?"

"Yes , mother."

I felt today that naval was always right and I was wrong.

***

CHAPTER EIGHT

Transformation

How many times I have told you , Raju , not to go there. They are low caste people. It doesn't look nice for us to mix with them.

"But , Mother ---- "

"No if or but. " Scolding , mother went to her office , father had departed half an hour before. School time is 10 O'clock so he had to remain alone for about two hours. He spends this time with Gita Didi playingwith her or asking questions. She stayed in the neighbourhood only. But don't know why mother feels bad about it.

Today Raju did not go to meet Geeta Didi. He was sitting sadly and waiting for parents to return from office. But again and again he desired to talk to Didi. How nice she is ! Everyday she gives him flower of Tuberose and talked to him very gently. She played with him like children. But why mother -----.

" Raju ---------"

Hearing the voice Raju turned and saw that Didi was standing at the door. He ran and clanged to her. " Didi I was remembering you. Againand again, I was thinking to go to you and listen to the fairy tale."

" They why didn't you come ? I was waiting for you and see I have Myself come to meet you. Come on , I will tell you story of red fairy."

Didi had just started telling the story when mother came. Raju was fearful and stopped her in the middle.

" Raju , where are you ? See , I have brought many toys for you." But no sooner did she see Didi , there was an angry frown on her face.

" You ! here ! "

Mother's love changed into anger and she said , " You want to be equal to us ! Remain in your limits , Geeta !"

Never try to persuade Raju. Got it ?

Geeta went away from there with tears in her eyes.

It was evening time Geeta was working Infront of her house when two strangers came enquiring about the house of Mr Sharma.

She pointed towards their house and said , "But there is no one in the house. Both husband and wife have gone to office and Raju has gone to school."

" Actually , Raju has met with an accident. We have come here with the help of identity card in his pocket. His very serious. We have admitted him in Gandhi Hospital. He is in a serious condition."

Geeta was deeply shocked. Taking down address of the hospital on a paper and posting it their door she rushed to the hospital. Seeing Raju's condition, she burst out in tears. " My dear brother. How all this happened ?"

Raju's parents too arrived. Geeta got aside seeing them.

"Mr. Sharma Raju needs blood , but unfortunately, we do not have this blood group in our blood bank. What is your blood group ?" Doctor asked in a worry.

" B group sir "

" Oh ! then you have to arrange from somewhere otherwise Raju may lose his life."

Geeta came forward saying , "Don't say so doctor. You may test my blood group. "

Fortunately, her blood group matched and his life was saved. As soon as he came to senses he called for Geeta Didi and not seeing her there , he fainted again.

Raju's mother called Geeta " Where are you going ? Your brother Raju needs you. Come here."

Geeta could not believe her ears. " But Madam , I am a low ------ ! "

" No dear till today I was in dark . I believed in caste discrimination. But today you saved my son's life by giving blood. I have understood that man's identity is not his caste , but behaviour. Excuse me for my wrong behaviour."

***

CHAPTER NINE

FRAGRANCE OF RELATIONSHIP

I kept the newspaper aside and went to the gate. It was postman who handed me a marriage invitation card. I read the name in shining letters, Urmi Garg, again and again. I could not believe my eyes, same name, same village. At once an incident of about one and half year ago came before my eyes.

Mr. and Mrs. Atul Garg were our neighbour. His younger brother, Vipul, also lived with them and studying. We two families were so close to each other, as if we were a single family. After our husbands, Rohit and Mr. Atul, went to office, we two ladies got busy in gossiping and knitting sweaters. We could not live without each other. Returning from the college, Vipul also played with children. Children also played calling Uncle, uncle!!

After education, Vipul also got job. His marriage was also fixed. Pratibha gave me the card of Vipul's marriage and requested to attend.

The girl's family belonged to village, so they went to their village 10 days before the marriage. We too reached one day before with family to attend the marriage. the function was well organised. All were happy to see beautiful gentle daughter-in-law.

After sometime, Mr. Atul was transferred to some other place. He was concerned about his brother Vipul. But we assured him that Vipul is our brother too, so he could stay with us. He used to go to office in the morning and return in the evening.

One day Vipul informed that he was transferred to some other place. So he left the place. He expressed his obligations to us for the time he spent with us and promised to come time to time.

After sometime he came with his wife Urmi and to give me a surprise, kept her away and came alone om the door. I asked, "Why didn't you bring Urmi?"

Very innocently, holding his ears, indicated towards her. She came and touched my feet. I embraced her warmly.

While going Urmi said pleadingly, "Didi, you too come soon someday. At least see how we are living."

Complaining about Vipul she said, "Didi, he drives very fast. I have told him many times, but he never listens to me."

Many times I too had scolded him for this, but he always said, "What should I do, sister, as much I try to slow it down, it moves faster. Death is certain sister, and it will come on time so what is there to take tension. Death time can never be postponed."

His philosophical talks made me speechless.

It was holiday. We all were sitting in the lawn. Just then telephone bell rang. I received the call. It was some unknown voice.

"Hello, 7369, please!"

"Yes, speaking!"

"Do you know Vipul Garg?"

"Yes, very well. What happened to him?" I asked anxiously.

"Actually,Vipul has met with an accident. I am his friend. I got your number from Vipul's wife."

I enquired the name of hospital , ward number and bed number and kept the receiver. We were in a great anxiety, imagining his condition. I didn't like to talk to anyone. Rohit was also looking at the watch again and again one minute seemed like an age.

Reaching the hospital, we reached the emergency ward. Vipul had already been taken to the operation theatre. Urmiclanged to me weeping bitterly as soon as she saw me.

Controlling myself I tried to console Urmi " Don't cry dear, bebrave , everything will be Ok."

The whole night we kept waiting for the doctor to come out of the operation theatre and give us some comforting news. But the whole night passed Vipul's parents and Mr. Atul and his wife all had come by that time seeing them Urmi started weeping bitterly.Suddenly the door of operation theatre opened and doctor came out saying " Sorry , we could not save Vipul Inspite of all our efforts."

It was a bolt from the blue. Urmi stood like a stone statue continuously staring towards the operation theatre. Everyone started weeping bitterly. There was no one to console anyone.

After Vipul's death , Urmi was persistently moving towards depression and then Mr Atul and his wife asked us for suggestions and I suggested for her remarriage. At this both became violent.

" What are you saying sister ? Will our society accept it ? Father is conservative. He will never accept it."

" I will persuade him" I said. Both laughed in chorus and said , " You are thinking of turning a stone into wax and even if he agrees , who is there in her parent's house to perform the ceremony.Her mother had died in her childhood and father and step mother also died in a car accident after the marriage. She has one step brother , who is least concern about her."

I took a deep sigh and kept quiet but I could not control myself and reached Vipul's village , after some days with my husband and children. We were not stranger to Vipul's parents , but my suggestion vexed him and he stared at me as if he would turn me into ashes.

" You all have gone mad. You have forgotten all the limits of respect and discipline. The whole village will mock at us."

Hearing him , Rohit looked at me amazingly. But I tried to convince him. Urmi is still very young and criticized the conservative customs of society , but nothing affected him. Persuading him was a hard nut to crack.

Suddenly a paper slipped out from the middle of the card. And I came out of my nostalgic mood. I picked up the paper , it was the letter of Atul's father. I read with an amazement –

Dear Daughter I beg excuse for that day when I talked to you harshly. But later I realized that each word seemed a reality we really destroy many innocent lives being tied in the conservative tradition. God has taken away my son. Should I deprive myself of daughter's love too. No , No , whatever the society thinks , I will myself do the kanyadan of Urmi. You must come."

Your fatherPrem Kumar Garg

Drops of tear felt from my eyes on the letter. It expressed my joy and fragrance of a new relation entered my heart and soul.

***

CHAPTER TEN

OWN LIMITS

"Neha , what's the matter you have not been doing your home work for many days ?"

"Mam , mother is not at home."

" Where has she gone ?"

" Don't know mam."she said innocently

" Don't know ! means ! " A doubt got in my mind. At the same time I felt angry too for carelessness of her parents

" OK, come with your father tomorrow"

" Yes Mam."

The next day I had just come and taken my place in principal's office after inspecting all the classes when the peon informed.

" Someone has come to meet you."

"Send him inside."

Just as the visitor entered the office, I was shocked to see him and " You ! " slipped from my mouth.

The visitor too looked at me in surprise.

I tried to be normal and said , " Yes " , what do you want ?"

" Mam , my daughter, Neha , had told that -----"

" Oh ! Neha is your daughter?"

Suddenly some past events surrounded my mind.

It was 10 O'clock in the night , I was just going to lock the door. when I heard a knock. Who can be there at this hour? I thought. Mother went to open the door and I tried to trace the person from inside.

"Oh ! You ! come , come !" Mother said joyfully.

After wishing mother , the visitor asked about father.

" Yes , yes , he is sleeping inside. I am waking him up. You just be seated ." Mother movedtowards the bedroom and the man sat on the chair in the lobby. I peeped from the door. By the time father had also come.

" Wow ! after such a long time ! how did you turn this way ?"

" I had just come for some work. So, I thought of meeting you."

" Can I have your introduction ?"

Father asked the young man sitting near.

" He is my nephew. He is English lecturer in a college in Poona. I had talked to you about this chap only."

" What's your name ?"

" Tushar."

I viewed from inside the door and said to myself. " Oh ! uncle was praising Tushar only , that day." Strong physique , wheatish complexion and attractive personality , after talking for sometime uncle made a move saying – " Now Tushar will meet you from time to time."

Mother , Father went to bedroom. Papa was telling , " how did you like the boy ?"

" Nice , I just wish that they appreciate our daughter and we come to know about their demand."

Father instructed mother , " Don't tell Ranjana anything about it. Next time when he comes, we can arrange their meeting."

About Six months passed. I had almost forgotten the matter. That day we brothers and sisters were reading and parents were not at home, when the call bell rang. I went and opened the door. A woman , middle aged was standing at the door. I wished her and looked at her intently.

" Excuse me, I am unable to recognize you."

" How can you ? You have never seen me. I am Tushar's mother. He was not in his Quarter. I got your addressfrom his boss."

" Yes, please do come in." We gave her a chair to sit.

Casting her eyes in all direction , she asked, " Where are your parents ?"

"They have gone out for some work. Have you to say anything ?"

My question made her look a bit serious. " Tushar's younger brother is admitted in the medical here. He is suffering from Encephalitis."

" Don'tworry.My parents will come tomorrow."

Next day Mummy – Papa came back. I informed them everything. Now we cooked patient's food every day and my younger brother carried it to the hospital.

After some days Prasarwas discharged from the hospital. They all come to our house.

" Listen, this girl will be suitable for our Tushar."

Hearing these words from uncle to aunty, I blushed and rushed inside after serving them food.

One week later we received a letter from Tushar's father. It was full of praise for me. Mummy and papa were very happy. On the 5th day Tushar came. As per mother's instruction. I took tea to Tushar , I was about to turn back when Tushar Asked.

" What's your name ?"

" Ranjana."

" What are you doing now a days ?"

" M.A in English."

" My parents were praising you a lot."

I was thrilled to hear the statement.

Just then mother entered asking him, " That's why I am asking your view about marriage."

" What shouldI say aunty ? My parents want that I should marry soon , but I have no wish at all to marry. If I Marry, I would prefer a service holder girl. You know in present condition one income cannot meet all our demands."

Mother had not expected such a reply from Tushar "It's your view. But wife looks ornamental at home. So many tensions come up. There remains no closeness."

But Tushar presented his explanations to emphasise his opinion.

" But my Ranjanais against service."

Tushar asked , " Why ?" When I nodded in favour.

"Because first duty of a lady is to take care of her family , her house , that is the world of her dream. These things are not possible with service."

He commenced slowly , " Everyone has his own opinion."

Hence, I was married somewhere else. The house of my in laws was very big. Mother-in-law used to run school in one part of the house. Since last two weeks she was not well so I had to manage everything.

" Madam , you had ------"

" Yes , I had called you. Take your seat." I moved to present.

He casted his eyes all around and not finding anyone there he became comfortable and said,

" Ranjana Ji , I am much ashamed. What can I do ? My wife is a service holder. But I never got peace of mind you were quite right. Woman's duty is to take care of the family but this is not possible along with service.She preferred to take divorce to leaving job."

" But you ------ service."

" No Tushar , I have a prosperous family my husband is as per my attitude and I am not on job here. This is our own school. "

***

CHAPTER ELEVEN

After Dark Night

Fire broke out rapidly all around me and I was trying to call for help, but due to , dread my voice gotchoked. I tried to cry out and immediately a cry escaped from my mouth.

"Save ! Save ! Save me ! fire ! fire !"

"Rama ! Rama ! what happened ? Had you a nightmare ?" Anant shook me with force.

My heart was beating very fast holding Anant's hand in mine I asked , "Shall I ever be able to come out of this stigma Anant ?"

" You are free dear. You worry uselessly." Just sleep. He put his arms below my head.

After a while Anant drifted into sleep but there was no sleep in my eyes. Lying on the bed I was thinking about the past and comparing it with present. Today I have all the happiness of life, loving, husband , post , wealth , respect and everything. But the darkness of past palls the golden colour of today.

I was about five years old. My father was a tyrant and always mistreated mother. My brother elder to me and sister , Ananya Younger to me and I myself too were always terrified before father.

Father drank , gambled and came home late in the night , abused everyone and beat us. We all used to wake up by his harsh voice. There was a hue and cry in the whole house until he slept. It was a daily routine. Not only this he never told anything to brother even after mother made so many complaints against him about his mischievous activities. That's why mother lost her value in his eyes. He took him more as a servant than a mother. There was no use of telling anything to father. Even if I tried , I had to tolerate scolding and beating of brother.

" Stop, you, Idiot , if you have so much concern for mother. Why don't you do all her work ?"

That day he crossed all the limits. He poured tea leave in the whole milk. When father came at night and asked for milk. Mother gave him the same tea mixed milk. He threw that hot tea over mother in anger.

The next day he repeated his action and, on my objection, he beat me too much. We mother and daughter lived merrily when father and brother were not in the house, but as soon as they entered the house, we got frightened.

Brother too turned like father.With the support of mother I completed my M.A. and then B.Ed. in first division. I met Anant during my college days only but never revealed due to the fear of father and brother.

After B.Ed. , father married me to Vikky , the son of one of his colleagues. But I could not open my mouth and came to my in-law's house. Anant had gone abroad for higher studies , so he had no idea about this marriage.

I had completed B.Ed. , so I got a job in college on a good salary. Everything was quite normal in the beginning. I tried to forget Anant and engage myself in my house. I felt everyone was affectionate for me, but later I discovered that it was an illusion.

One day family ofmy husband's friend came to meet me and enquired about the dowry he got in the marriage.

" In marriage I have got beautiful Rupaji and the empty corner in the room is waiting for the dining table her father has promised and that corner for refrigerator. Ten months have passed. Let us see when ---------"

" It'sOK then we shall see it later" and they went away. But now I started feeling the spark of hatred for him in my mind. Everyone's behaviour towards me changed . Vikky started hating me.

Now I was insulted before everyone. Many times, days passed without eating anything. But I never informed about it to father.

My health deteriorates due to a lot of work and no food. Falling down due to dizziness became common. I could not go to college. This became a cause of greater tension.

One day at night I got up to open the door and fell down. Mother -in-law opened the door. It was Vikky , badly drunk. He came and fell on the bed.

" O. beautiful, bring a glass of water." said Vikky in a wobbling voice.

" See , I am unable to walk , don't know what has happened in my leg." I said helplessly.

"Shameless ! making excuses !" Vikky started beating me badly and then went out of the room. I remembered mother. I wrote a letter to mother and gave a letter to a boy in the neighbourhood to post and consoled myself.

It was raining heavily and growing dark. Vikky had not returned since yesterday. At about 8 O'clock a rickshaw stopped in front of my house. It was Vikky with a stranger. We brought Vikky inside and with the help of the stranger lay him on the sofa.

" Oh ! what happened !" Mother came shouting.

" He was badly drunk and lying on the road. I happened to cross from there and carried him to you otherwise anything could have happened." said the stranger.

" It is all because of you , shameless !" with these words his mother started crying.

I was shocked to see the stranger. He was Anant himself.

" You ! in this condition , Ruma !" He asked.

Vikky was laying senseless. Hours passed , but there was no improvement. In the morning doctor came and declared him dead.

My parents too were crying badly at my life and took me with them, after coming back home, Anant took me to a doctor. Doctor checked me up. Haemoglobin was very low. But with regular treatment I recovered.

One day father asked me , "Ruma , do you know Anant. Will he be nice match for Ananya ? "

" Very nice !" I said without giving any thought.

" You ask Anant about this proposal."

" OK I will ask him."

When I put this proposal before Anant , he got angry.

" No Ruma , never,I cannot think of anyone else besides you." He spoke frankly.

"But I.............."

" That's enough. Don't speak further."

"You have alreadysuffered so much. Now I won't let you suffer anymore. Anaya will get many nice proposals. But I will never get my Ruma."

Anant filled my colourless life with beautiful colours. But the terrible past clouded my mind many times and I cried in sleep.

But Anant's affection always brought me out of my dark past.

" Don't fear , Ruma. I am with you." ***

CHAPTER TWELVE

INNOCENT

Mother's letter had put me in a dilemma. I was unable to decide what to do. The lines in the letter were emerging like a whirlpool in the mind. The more I read the letter, the more tense I became. I read the letter again

" Dear son. We have fixed your marriage. Engagement ceremony is on 20th and marriage after 10 days. So take a leave and come soon. "

This was not the first letter on the matter. Two years before also mother had posted me such a letter. It was full of the promise of girl and her family. I was very happy to read it. I was mad with joy. Actually, I was tired of bachelor life and wanted some partner with whom I could share my joys and sorrow.

I had drawn a picture of the girl from the letter of mother and I always dreamt of my life with her.Friends also started making preparation to go in the marriage procession. In the next letter mother sent her photograph. I was crazy she was really very beautiful. I kept her photograph in my wallet and at night under my pillow.

Once my friend Ganesh tried to crack a joke and he took away her photograph from my wallet. I got angry over him. " Why are you so vexed. Only eightdays are left. You will meet her in reality." Ganesh commented and handed me the photograph.

I got irritated and said , " Where did you get it ?"

" Under the pillow , when I was giving the bedsheet and pillow cover to the washerman. " And he started for office.

I too packed my suitcase and caught train at eight O'clock and reached home. I was very happy I felt as if every free , beds full of flowers , greenfield rivers all were greeting mejoyfully.

At home , everyday , there was some or other ritual. Sisters in law made jokes and at last the day came when I reached her home with the marriage procession.

She came on the stage, looking very beautiful among the flowers with a flower garland in her hand and put it around my neck. I was lost in her beauty my dream broke when my friend pushed me. I too put the garland around her neck. There was a big clapping in the pandal. Then continued many rituals throughout the night.

We reached back to our house. Many relatives were eagerly waiting for the new bride. The whole day was spent in rituals and then came the precious moment to meet my life partner.Unveiling her I saw her beautiful face and was thrilled to see the moonlike beauty and spoke out, " I am blessed to get such a beautiful life partner."

"I am more blessed than you.You are God , you have accepted me Inspite of knowing all the facts about my life "

Her words brought me out of my toxication and asked her , " What ! What facts you are talking of ? I don't know anything about you. Tell me everything clearly."

Poonam was quite afraid to see my changed disguise and with tears in her eyes , she asked surprisingly , " What? you don't know anything about me ? But I was told that you have promised to accept me Inspite of having every information about me."

"Accident ! what accident ? But I am totally unaware of any dark fact about your life."

She narrated all the story of her life , weeping. She told , " I was only two years old. My mother went to visit her suffering sister. The neighbour misbehaved with me. I started crying. The neighbours collected and got that person arrested. I was taken to the hospital in an unconscious state."

Saying all this she looked at me helplessly as if she wanted to ask what her fault was. But I became stone hearted and did not listen to her.

" No , I can't accept you after knowing all these things. I am not a social reformer." saying this I rushed out of the room in anger.

But laterI came to know that my parents knew everything about it. But perhaps due to the greed of dowry or three daughters to be married. I don't know why they didn't tell me anything about it. The more I thought the more I was confused.

Poonam never came back to in-law's house again. Though I knew she was innocent , But the fire burning inside my heart burnt all me desires into ashes. Many times, I got seriously ill but never called her. My friend Ganesh tried to convince me many times.

Perhaps I too could never forget her tear full eyes. I always thought where was her fault ? But I was never ready to withdraw. Her parents too come to me pleadingly but I never answered but my anger was against whom ? Was it against Poonam or that culprit neighbour or against the system of society ? I was unable to decide.

But today I received mother's letter for my marriage , the memory of Poonam , became fresh in my mind. Her words -----. "What is my fault ? tell me , what is my fault ? "

startedhammering my mind.

The whole night passed without sleep , tossing in the bed. Wherever I tried to sleep her tearful face came before my eyes I became restlessness.

In the morning , with the chirping of birds and rising sun, I left the bed. Being free from daily routine. I become ready and started my journey to bring Poonam back. I sent a wire to mother " Mother , your son will no more wander. He is going to bring his Poonam back."

CHAPTER THIRTEEN

SOLUTION

" Brother , I shall not be able bear the burden of both of them."

" But brother, mother and father both want to live together."

"Then why don't you keep both of them with you ?" The younger one said in anger.

"Brother-in-law , you have only two sons. But we have daughters. We have to arrange for their marriage too. How will it be possible ?"

This word reached the ears of mother passing from there. Their words started hammering her brain. Laid down on her bed. Like a lifeless tree. There was no sleep in her eyes. She looked at the innocent face of her husband sleeping beside her. He does not even know that we have become a burden for our children and felt like waking him up and telling him the deeds of her sons.

Whenever she used to say to her husband to think about their future , he always used to say " Radha , why should we worry ? We have to sons like diamond."

Her eyes got teary and started thinking. Always sacrificed for the joy of both sons. He always tried to satisfy all their demand. Always tried to provide him best education , food , clothes and everything they needed. They can't even imagine how hard we tried to provide them high post , respect and reputation. They are treating us this way ! Now we have become a burden on them !

We distributed everything equally between the two – home , property. Now they are diving us !

She came out of her thoughts with the voice of the guard outside " Keep awaken! keep awaken!" She saw towards the clock. It was fifteen minutes past three. All the vein of the brain started stretching. She tried to reduce her tension pressing her forehead.

The monotony of the environment was now and then broken by the voice of the guard. But the violent storm of her mind was not ceasing. She was in a great dilemma. Just thenher husband called out , " Radha , give me some water. " And she got up.

"What's the problem , Radha ? You are still lying awake ?"

"Nothing." she said hiding her sorrow.

" OK, What's the time ?"

"Four O'clock." lighting the torch towards the clock she replied.

He again slept in a sound sleep. He was unaware of the fact that the sons whom he thought diamond , proved the pieces of glass. She could not remember a single moment whenthey had ever neglected their children.

She recalled the day when their school was going on a tour to Shimla. It was the last week of month and there was not sufficientmoney in the house. I told Shyam that we can cancel their programme , making them aware of the programme. Shyam laughed and said generally , " No, Radha. We are earning only for the joy of children. They will be hurt. Don't worry. I shall make some arrangement. Don't deny them for the tour."

Many times, in life we sacrificed for their joy. Today these children have no care for us. How to make them understand that we cannot live without each other. We have strong spiritual bond. We always prayed God that he might keep our bond alive till the last breath. Now my sons are making a conspiracy against it.

" No , I shall not let them do any such thing. I will not listen to Shyam also. I cannot ever dream of living separately. Shame on such children , who cannot think of their parents' happiness."

It was morning Shyam woke up and seeing me he asked , " What happened Radha ? Why are your eyes red and swollen ? It seems you have been awake the whole night ? Tell me ?"

"Nothing." I tried to hide but could not and blurt out. And narrated every fact that I had suffered the whole night.

He too became a bit tensed for a moment but the next moment became normal and said , "That's all ! you have gone mad. You should not mind these things. They are children afterall!"

"Children ! They are no more children now. You also do wonders. They are father of two – three children." I said in anger.

" You are really innocent , Radha . They too love us very much as we love them."

" You mean , whatever I heard was my Illusion ? It was all a lie ?"

" I don't mean so, but think seriously. Things are very costly now-a -days and it is very heavy to carry the burden of a family.Our timewas different. One person earned and the whole family depended on him. But today the time is very different. Besides expense of children's education, their marriage and so many other expenses."

His words gave me some comfort.

" But this doesn't mean that children should divide parents. They have taken us as propertywhich can be divided."

" This will never happen , Radha. We shall never live separately. Let us go on pilgrimage.Before our children announce their decision we must declare ours. We shall live in some ashram ! "

"No , father , don'tdo this. Please excuse us both of you will live together wherever you live, All the four sons and daughters- in- law touched their feet and felt sorry.

Shyam's eyes were filled with the tears of joy and he said " No dear , you all live here happily. Let us do what we have decided. Don't stop us from this good deed. We shall contact and talk to you from time to time."

***

CHAPTER FOURTEEN

Shades of Life

Like other days I had hardly come from the office and sat on the chair when Achala handed me two letters.

After turning the letters , I first opened the longer envelop and brought out the paper inside it.

“Oh ! Achala , your marksheet !” Achala came running and taking the Marksheet from my hand started reading it. Then I took up the other letter and opened it. I was shocked to see the shining card inside the envelop. I was full of jealousy and anger. For a moment the taste of mouth become sour and many sweet memories of past started changing into enmity. The incidents of twenty years before become alive on mind.

Mr Suresh was our new neighbour. These was no one else except husband and wife in there house. My husband invited them on dinner. I enjoyed talking to his wife Rekha.we started coming closer. Mr.Vashishtha was manager in the bank and my husband was assistant manager in the same bank. There was a great similarly in their work as well as nature. The whole day they remained together in the bank and in the evening,they had a long sitting of chess and both of us were tired of waiting for them on the dining table. Neither of us had any child to entertain us with his sweet talks. So, we got angry over our husbands.

" It's a limit. The whole day we wait for the evening that in the evening we shall go to market and both of you get busy with your chess and forget the whole world." But we did not get any response from their side except ' Hmm'. Their attention was towards chess board. As if they were going to become king , winning the game.

We used to become angry and the got busy in our gossip. Usually, we had our dinner either in their house or ours. Myself and Rekha cooked the dinner together. This was our daily routine.

One day we were gossiping when Rekha suddenly had a feeling of nausea. We took her to the doctor .it was diagnosed that she was pregnant. There was a difference of One and half month between her and my pregnancy. All were very happy.

One day all of us were sitting. Our husbands busy playing the chess. Mr Garg's attention was diverted and my husband took the chance. Mr Garg said , " This is the speciality of this game. As soon as your attention gets diverted , you lose it. Just now a thought came to my mind."

My husband , still busy in his game said , "first you save your soldier."

" First time a thought has struck my mind and you are not allowing me to speak. "

My husband called both of us too to come near.

Rekha asked her husband , "Tell what you are trying to tell ?"

At this my husband reacted promptly , " What will he say sister-in-law ? I have surrounded his king. Now he is trying to escape the problem by turning talks."

I spoke out angrily , " You just don't see anything besides chess. Tell brother what were you telling ?"

" Just now a thought come to my mind that one of you give birth to a male child and other to a girl child. We shall marry both of them when they grow older."

" Oh ! what !"

Suddenly Mr. Gupta Spoke out as if coming out of his intoxication of chess , " sure ?"

Mr Garg said smiling , " Hundred percent sure."

All of us smiled looking at each other with a sort of affirmations in our minds.

That day it was raining very heavily. It was a dark night. Mr Garg had gone out of station for some official work Rekha was in my home only. Suddenly she had labour pain. We took her to the nursing home. After admitting her , we sat outside the room on a bench , hoping for a successful delivery. But after sometime nurse came out of the room and said , " She needs an operation .Call her husband to signthe agreement paper.

We were in a dilemma and explained that her husband was out of station for 4 to 5 days. But as she explained the emergency, I took the form and signed it myself. We were very anxiously lingering near the operation theatre. Our eyes were towards it when the nurse come and informed that the patient needed blood of O positive group.

After about one and a half hour the door of operation theatre opened. Doctor came out but without saying anything he moved ahead. We were in a state of anxiety but did not dare to ask him anything. Just then nurse came out and made us happy by giving the news that Rekha had given birth to a male child. Mother and child both were quite well and we might meet them.

As we entered the room Rekha's eyes became teary. " What would have happened to my child if you were not there with me ?"

" Rekha" I patted her lovingly.

"Deepa if you give birth to a girl child. She will be my daughter in law. "

"Leave it Rekha. Who has seen the future?

It is my word. I may write it on a stamp paper " Rekha confirmed.

Everything went on as we had thought I was blessed with a girl child a month later. Rekha's son was Achal so we named our daughter Achala. We all enjoyed theirinnocent activities. Our life was moving on pleasantly and children were growing up. But nobody knows what's going to happen the next. One day myself and Rekha were gossiping and enjoying children's activities. Just then a peon , Raju came from bank. He was panting badly. we were anxious to see his condition. I asked him , " What happened , Raju ? What's the problem ? "

" What to say Madam. There was a robbery in the bank today. Mr Gupta left us forever and Mr Garg is in the hospital in a wounded state. "

I stood like a statue. Now we two - mother and daughter were completely alone in the world. I got the job in my husband's place. I used to leave my daughter with Rekha. But this support was also withdrawn when Mr Garg was transferred after sometime.

In the beginning we corresponded but after some years our correspondence became very rare. Everyone forgot us with the passage of time. These letters added ansalt to injury.

" What's the matter, maa ? Why do you look so worried ?" Achala's words made me conscious and I tried to be normal wiping sweat on my face.

" Ok , you just wash your face. I am preparing some tea for you. "

After Achala moved towards the kitchen. I opened the invitation card. I read , " You are invited with family on the naming ceremony of their son."

" Oh , Achal has been married and has got a son too. Rekha forgot her promise she was to write It ona stamp paper." I was filled with resentment.

" Did not even invite me in her son's marriage?Was my daughter not worthy of her son ? Yes! Why will she join relation with us ? After all, Achala is daughter of a widow!" I would have continued murmuring had Achala not came with a cup of tea.

I decided and the next day I reached there with Achala. Rekha embraced me lovingly as she saw us.

"Oh ! our Achala has grown up into a beautiful lady ! far better in beauty than her mother !"

Neglecting her words , I asked " Where is Achal's wife and her son ?"

"Achal's wife ? her son ? what are you telling Rekha ?"

I got irritated and extended the card towards her. "Is this a false news?"

" No , this is hundred percent true ?"

" Then ?"

"What then ? have you gone mad. We didn't meet for such a long time but it doesn't mean that I have forgotten my promise. Achal is doing engineering in London. He is for Achala and will be hers."

Rekha's sentences seemed a puzzle to me. Rekha laughed and said " Now I have understood your confusion. Actually,my husband's elder brother and his wife died leaving a son. It is the naming ceremony of his son , son of Avinash , that you have misunderstood and showing your anger on me."

I was ashamed and embracing Rekha I cried bitterly and I could only utter " Excuse me Rekha."

***

CHAPTER FIFTEEN

BETTER LATE THAN NEVER

My feet moved very fast seeing the car standing outside the gate. I came upto the yard but as the conversation going inthe inside reached my ears, my steps stopped and I kept standing there.

" You just don't worry about me, Kavita is here. She will take my care. I have separated them so that I would always have a support in old age otherwise -------"

Mother's words pierced my ears like an arrow. Feet got stuck to the ground. But controlling myself I entered into the room.

" O ! Kamini , how are you ? Is everything OK ?" I said embracing her.

" Everything is OK." Kamini said managing her saree and after having some snacks she started to go and I stopped her " Why are you going so early ? You may go in the morning we have not yet have enough conversation."

" No sister , I will come some other time. I had told my mother- in- law that I would return by evening. I am already late everyone will worry."

" It's alright dear. You must go. Your in-laws have more right on you than we." Mother said and then Kamini left wishing everyone and the car moved.

I and mother came inside sadly. Mother was sad as Kamini had just left , and I was troubled due to what I had heard mother saying. I could not help and asked " Why did you do so mother? Just because of your selfish aim ? You didn't even think about me ?"

She laid down on the bed tying her head with a handkerchief. I felt very aggressive. As if I am never tired but I had never spoken against her so today also I remained silent and started preparing dinner. So many thoughts started coming to my mind.

Had I not heard mother that time and would have listened to in-laws , I would not have been in such a miserable condition. I came into her spell and without thinking about my right and wrong , left in-laws house and came here. But no use crying over the spilt milk. I have to reap whatever I have sown.

After preparing food served it to mother and I myself had my dinner then I went to bed. Sleep was very far from my eyes. Standing on the counter the whole day made me tired , then mother's words were making me restless. Why did mother do so ? How can mother treat her two daughters differently ? Why did she marry me then? Only to make a way for Kamini's marriage ? She had sent me to my in-laws-house with such a spirit , so that I could never judge her clever tricks. But I too had lost my wit that time.

Since the beginning I was introvert in nature. I had to obey her in every condition. It became My habit to listen to all her orders. Kamini was of independent nature since the beginning. She always acted as per her wish. Mother too didn't say anything to her. Father died when I was fourteen. His pension was our source of living. Kamini was in intermediate. I had completed my M.A. in economics privately and had got the job of a clerk in bank.

One day father's cousin sister brought a proposal. The boy was engineer in a department everything was perfectly OK like- house, family etc. preparation of marriage started. I came to in laws house full of dreams and hopes. There also I got much affection. My husband , Rajesh , was a man of self-respect. Though we were in the same town , he did not like to go to my parent's house often. One day I went to my parent's house promising to come back in the evening but mother did not allow to come.

Rajesh reached there in the evening indignant. " Kavita why don't you understand ? You stayed here without any information. Do you realise how worried we all got when you didn't reach home ? "

I was a bit afraid and in fear I spoke " I had told mother Though she had gone to Haridwar in the morning." Rajesh got very angry on my lie.

I kept quiet mother got angry and told , "Listen Rakesh , I have not sold you my daughter. How can you talk to her like this ?"

"That is not the point mother. But she should have at least informed us."

" Why should she inform everything ? She is not your slave. Why don't you alsocame and live here with Kavita ?"

At this Rajesh got angry and said , "Won't you come with me , Kavita ?"

I was silent. I looked down when he did not get any answer, he moved.

I cried when Rajesh went away. Mother said . " Why are you weeping ? He will himself come when you won't go for two to three days. He will himself agree to stay here. Don't worry at all,my child."

I very well knew that he would never come. But it was difficult to explain her everything. Months passed there was no information from Rajesh. Many times, I tried to go but she always stopped me. Meanwhile I got busy in making arrangement for my unwise mother and Kamini. Mother and Kamini became my duty.

After sometimes Kamini was married. Mother never stopped her from doing her duty towards her in-laws. She always guided her in right direction. But why did she behave adversely with me? Because she was worried about her old age? But it was my fault that I took the wrong decision.

The alarm clock made me conscious. When the whole night passed , I don't know. I had a severe headache.

In the morning I started for office but my feet turned towards Rajesh's house. I pressed the call bell, a child of four years came out. I was deeply surprised to see the boy and started thinking if he were the son of Rajesh. But I asked " Dear son , What's your father's name ?"

" Rajesh."

His answer was a shock for me. Now it was confirmedthat Rajesh has married and now it's not proper for me to stay here. I was about to turn when Rajesh's sister Geeta saw me.

"Kavita Bhabhi ! you ! Come in why are you standing apart ?"

I went in and sat on the sofa. My eyes were searching something Gita Guessed " What are you searching sister-in-law ? Brother is about to come."

" No ,not that, where is his Wife ?"

" Wife ? whose wife ? who are you then ?"

" I mean the child. He told me that his father's name is Rajesh."

" Yes, Kavita his father's name is also Rajesh."

Just then Rajesh entered the room saying , " He is the son of your sister-in-law , Neeta."

Knowing the truth, I fell into his feet and cried bitterly.

" Please excuse me , Rajesh. I could not understand Mother's selfishness and ruined my family myself. Now I have realised my mistake."

" No Kavita , your place is safe in this house. You have understood what is right and is wrong." Better late than never.

***

CHAPTER SIXTEEN

SHORT STORIES 1- ILLITERATE

There was a function of some scholars under the presidentship of Mr Gupta on the subject “utility of education in daily life.”

About half an hour after the beginning of the programme , Mr Gupta came on his scooter and placing it carelessly in front of the board, he entered into the hall.

He was noticing everything very silently for some time , but could not remain silentany more , “ Why , brother scooter , is your master Illiterate ?” asked the ‘ No parking board ’.

***

CHAPTER SEVENTEEN

OPPORTUNITY

A sudden sound of blast opened his eyes. People were crying , shrieking and calling out for help. His eyes gleamed. Inspite of chill winter he left his bed of warm clothes and rushed in the direction of the noise. After many years he had got this opportunity again.

***

CHAPTER EIGHTEEN

BURDEN

I and my son Sagar were in a hurry to reach the station by short cut so that we might catch the train. It was early morning and light was very faint. I could not notice the pit and there was a sprain in my leg. It was very difficult to walk. But going was very urgent. Seeing me limping Sagar said , " Mother , give this bag to me otherwise we shall miss the train."

" No dear , bag is too heavy for you." Guessing the weight of the bag and looking at that small child , I said.

But he said , " No mother , give me the bag."

Holding the bag in his hand he said , " Wow mother , this is much lighter thanmy school bag."

***

CHAPTER NINETEEN

EFFECT OF COMPANY

All the ants moved in a proper Queue in the direction of food , on the information of a friend ant. In order to reach soon some of the ants got indiscipline and moved ahead breaking the queue , pushing one another.

Some of the ants did not like this behaviour of their friends, they said rebuking , " O ants ! behave yourself. Don't follow human beings for filling your belly."

***

CHAPTER TWENTY

RECOMMENDATION

Since morning there was a long queue of people coming in the temple and going out. The priest was sitting in the feet of God. Just then a beggar like man came inside the temple and begged to God in a miserable tone " O, God ! arrange for some Chapattis at least today , otherwise my son ------- I shall bow my head before you everyday." After sometimes a middle-aged man in ragged Kurta- Dhoti came inside. The man bowed his head and prayed to God. " O God ! you know everything. I am father of four daughters. I shall not be able to give so much dowry. Today a party is coming to see my elder daughter. Please God , fix everything at the lowest cost. I will offer you prasad of five rupees twenty-five paise."

Just then the priest saw that a very rich suited booted man come out of the car and entered the temple. He pleaded before God.

" O God ! do something that only the horse of number eight wins in the racing competition. Half of the money I win will be offered to you."

Hearing everyone's request to God the priest started thinking and prayed God , " O God , his horse of number eight should win."

***

CHAPTER TWENTY-ONE

THE SUPERIOR

News of Sapna's coming home created a hue and cry in the house. Mother was anxiously shouting over everyone in the house.

" Ratna , be quick , only two hours are left for Sapna to come. Ram has not yet come with the sweet."

Rohit could not see the restlessness of mother. He told, " What's the matter mother. All work will be finished in time. You are so much worried as if Sapna Didi is guest. She is our own. You never become so worried when Kamini Didi comes."

" You keep quiet. Talking uselessly. You must know that there is a great difference between Kamini and Sapana's in-laws-house."

" What is the difference ? I don't see any difference rather Kamini Didi's in-laws house is better than that of Sapana's. In Sapna Didi's house they are proudy and egoistic people." "That's why I say so. They are Superior people We have to take their greater care." Mother took a deep sigh.

***

CHAPTER TWENTY-TWO

RAPE

Five years old Sonu was busy in reading newspaper he called out his mother.

" Mother , the rapist is caught. He used to catch small girls and rape and kill them. What is rape mother ?" He asked thinking for a moment.

I was embarrassed. To satisfy his curiosity. I had to say something " Just to persuade small girls, taking them away and demanding something. If their demand is not fulfilled, they kill the girl. This is called Rape."

" No , mother , you don't know anything. " What you are explaining is kidnapping and murder."

His words made me speechless.

***

CHAPTER TWENTY-THREE

CURIOSITY

" Neha , O' Neha ! will you keep standing here or go to school ?" Neha shivered when her father roared , tying the knot of Tie.

" Just going papa , but --------"

"What is this but ? your mother has prepared some sandwiches , eat some and keep some in your lunch box. Got it ? I am going to office. I am getting late."

Little Neha was looking at him curiously and thinking if it was necessary for both of them to go to office.

***

CHAPTER TWENTY-FOUR

ALTERNATIVE

" Are you hearing ?"

" Yes , tell ."

"What's the date today ?"

" It's twenty.Was there any assignment for today ?"

" No , I was just thinking about the house hold things - pulse , spices and all other things ----- It is very difficult to manage in this less income ."

" Then ? should I start robbery?"

" I am not saying so. But Mr Gupta works in your office only. In their house ----- why don't you also -----------------"

" You Know it is very difficult to do everything being a principled man."

I Felt the gap widening in our relation since then.

***

CHAPTER TWENTY-FIVE

TATTLE

" Shyam's daughter- in- law is really great Inspite of being highly educated she has no proud. See our daughter- in- law . She is so proud of herself on this little education." Rama said with a deep sigh.

" Whatever you say. Your daughter- in- law looks educated. Shyam's daughter in law is not at all attractive. She always remains covered in veil. Doesn't speak even a word. Looks so inactive that one cannot say that she is educated."

***

CHAPTER TWENTY-SIX

RAKHI- THE SACRED THREAD

" Papa , why I don't have any sister?Bring me a sister. I will also get Rakhi tied on my wrist."

At the word ' Rakhi ' his face grew red and the letter of his sister shined before his eyes. "Brother, why do you send me money order on Rakhi ? I feel ashamed when anyone asks how much money has your brother sent. ?"

The child came closer and putting his hand around his father's neck he said again , " Please papa, bring me a sister. I will also send money order."

He could not control himself.

Wife came running hearing the sound of a slap , " What happened ?"

" Nothing , I just got angry." Then hid the letter controlling himself.

***

CHAPTER TWENTY-SEVEN

POWER OF FATE

“ Dear , Gardener had planted us at the same time with the same hands , then why did you remain so small and weak ?” Asked one plant to the other.

“ You are right , brother. But the gardener did not know that there were termite where he planted me.” The other plant said groaning.

***

CHAPTER TWENTY-EIGHT

UPBRINGING

After the whole day of exhausting work when I reached the bed at night. I saw my son Tapan, busy doing his homework. I turned my figures in his hair lovingly and looked at my husband sitting nearby.

Seeing towards me he said , " Today got very late from office."

" Both of you had to wait for long. I am really tried of this service. We shall such a daughter in law as will not be in any job."

Before I could finish my statement , Tapan spoke out , " No mother, I will marry a girl who is in job."

" Who will cook then ?"

" You when you went to office grand- mother used to cook food and do house hold work same way you will do then."

Statement of this small child compelled me to think.

***

CHAPTER TWENTY-NINE

ANXIETY

As daughter in law went inside the labour room , mother-in-law started praying God.

" O God ! please do not give female child to my daughter in law." The lady who had come with her said , " But sister there is no want of anything in your house. You have a lot of wealth. Only there is no girl in your house. Still, you do not want a girl child. Why ?"

" You don't know sister,In the earlier times we had to worry about girl's dowry and nice family. But now a days we see so many , heart touching incidents in the newspaper. So many difficulties emerge with girl since she is born." The lady said sadly.

***

CHAPTER THIRTY

OBLIGATION

I was tired of cleaning the grass lying here and there. But the birds made nest again and again.

I really felt sympathetic on the hard labour of the bird. But at the same time I was feeling irritated seeing the straws lying here and there. Seeing my irritation my maid servant suggested.

" Madam you keep a container for these birds. Then they will not scatter the Straws here and there."

I did the same. I kept one in the ventilator and really did not litter since then. They kept their nest in the box that I had kept. They chirped and seeing towards me they skimmed as if they were trying to show their obligation.

Printed by Libri Plureos GmbH in Hamburg, Germany